WEiRDO
HOPPING WEIRD! 12

Scholastic Press
345 Pacific Highway Lindfield NSW 2070
An imprint of Scholastic Australia Pty Limited (ABN 11 000 614 577)
PO Box 579 Gosford NSW 2250
www.scholastic.com.au

Part of the Scholastic Group
Sydney • Auckland • New York • Toronto • London • Mexico City
• New Delhi • Hong Kong • Buenos Aires • Puerto Rico

First published by Scholastic Australia in 2019.
Text copyright © Anh Do, 2019.
Illustrations copyright © Jules Faber, 2019.

All rights reserved. No part of this publication may be reproduced or transmitted in any form or by any means, electronic or mechanical, including photocopying, recording, storage in an information retrieval system, or otherwise, without the prior written permission of the publisher, unless specifically permitted under the Australian Copyright Act 1968 as amended.

A catalogue record for this book is available from the National Library of Australia

ISBN: 978-1-74299-792-6

Typeset in Grenadine MVB, Push Ups and Lunch Box.

Printed in China by RR Donnelley.
Scholastic Australia's policy, in association with RR Donnelley, is to use papers that are renewable and made efficiently from wood grown in responsibly managed forests, so as to minimise its environmental footprint.

10 9 8 7 6 5 4 3 2 1   19 20 21 22 23 / 1

ANH DO

Illustrated by JULES FABER

WEiRDO 12
HOPPING WEIRD!

A SCHOLASTIC PRESS BOOK
FROM SCHOLASTIC AUSTRALIA

ALL GOOOOOD!

CHAPTER 1

Mum has the <u>**COOLEST**</u> new job. She's a nurse at the animal hospital!

Lately, she's been bringing **sick animals** home to look after...

and we **all** like to help!

Last week, I showed Kenny the **koala** how to eat **gum leaves**.

LOOK, KENNY! GUMMY GUMMY, YUMMY YUMMY!

BLERK!

Sally fed milk to a baby **goat**.

ROW, ROW, ROW YOUR GOAT!

And Blockhead fed **MILK** to Roger.

WOOHOO!

Kenny the koala is all better now. His **sore ear** has completely **healed!**

ALL GOOOOOOOOD.

Now that he's **OK**, Mum has to take him back to the **wild**.

'He'll be very **happy** to be home again,' she said.

BUT FIRST, LET'S GET YOU KIDS TO SCHOOL!

We popped Kenny in a **comfy box** for the car ride. I held it on my lap.

'I hope you had fun at our house,' I said to Kenny. 'I liked **climbing trees** with you!'

YOU'RE A FUNNY-LOOKING KOALA!

'And it was **REALLY** funny when you **dressed up** in Roger's clothes,' said Sally.

But now it was time to say **goodbye**.

'Stay out of **trouble**,' said Sally.

'Bye, little guy!' I called from the **school gates**.

COME BACK AND VISIT ANY TIME!

HOP!
HOP!

CHAPTER 2

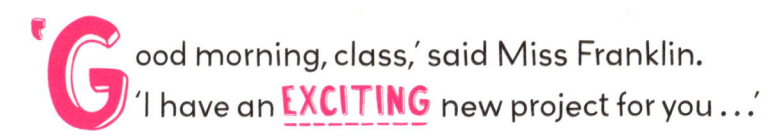

'Good morning, class,' said Miss Franklin. 'I have an **EXCITING** new project for you ...'

FILM-MAKING!

Film-making? **COOL!** That sounded **awesome!**

Miss Franklin told us that we'd be working in pairs, and we had to make a short film about **FRIENDSHIP**.

Straightaway, Henry turned to Wendy.

'Hey, Wendy,' he said. 'You love **cupcakes**. I love cupcakes. Want to make a film about **two friends** who love cupcakes?'

'Sure!' said Wendy.

'Weir,' said Bella. 'Want to be my partner?'

OF COURSE!

Bella and I make a really good team. I knew we'd come up with **something cool!** We always do!

But right now, we couldn't think of anything... even though we were trying **SUPER** hard!

THINKING, THINKING, THINKING... UGH!

After school, Bella came over so we could work on ideas. Dad suggested we have a 'brainstorm'.

A brainstorm?

BRRRRRR!

That wasn't working at all! It was just making me **cold!**

I stared at Bella. Bella stared at me. We had nothing! In fact, it was SO QUIET, you could hear a flea fart!

PARDON ME.

PFFFT!

'Hmm, **friendship**,' I said. 'Friend. Ship. I know! What about two … umm … **ships** that are **friends?**'

FRIEND SHIPS!

'*Friend* ships?' said Bella. 'I think we can do better than that …'

She was right, but coming up with ideas for the short film was **NOT** easy. Luckily, Mum came home with something **cool** to distract us!

'Hi, kids,' she said. 'We have a new house guest!'

THIS IS JOEY!

Our new guest was a **baby kangaroo!**

Joey was spotted alone in the bush. He'd hurt his foot trying to find his mum.

'Oh, that looks sore,' said Dad, patting Joey's foot. 'Does he need a ... **HOP-ERATION?**'

HA!

'No operations,' said Mum. 'He just needs some love and care until he's all **better** and **bouncing** around again.'

'Poor little guy,' said Bella, giving him a gentle scratch. 'He's **soooooo** cute!'

HI, JOEY.

'A koala, a goat, a joey ... you guys are **so** lucky!' said Bella.

It **was** pretty cool. It was almost like living in a **zoo!** You never knew what **animal** was going to show up next. Imagine a gorilla!

WHAT DO YOU FEED A 500 KILOGRAM GORILLA?

ANYTHING IT WANTS!

'What are you two working on?' said Mum.

'We have to make a **short film** about friendship,' said Bella. 'But we're having **trouble** coming up with ideas.'

GOOD IDEAS.

'Well,' said Mum, 'you have to film **SOMETHING**—anything's better than nothing. Maybe once you get started the **ideas** will come to you.'

That sounded good to us. I hoped she was right.

'I'm sure you'll work it out,' said Mum. 'Now, I know a **joey** who needs his blanket unwrapped and his **bandage** changed!'

YES, I'M TALKING ABOUT YOU, LITTLE ONE!

Seeing Mum with the roo gave me an idea. Maybe we could start **filming** Joey!

It didn't have anything to do with friendship... but at least it was a start. And I knew Bella would **love** the idea!

'Let's film Joey,' I said.

THAT'D BE AWESOME!

'Mum, can we film Joey?' I asked her. 'For our school project?'

'Sure thing!' she said. 'That sounds like fun.'

I held up the **phone** and started filming Mum changing Joey's bandage. It was good to practise all the different things the **camera** did. Like **zooming**.

OOPS! TOO CLOSE!

And **focusing**.

MONSTER!
OH, IT'S JUST JOEY.

And **special effects**.

WEIRD!

'But if I'm in it,' said Mum, 'make sure you get my **good** side.'

Her good side?
What did that mean?!

Good side.

Bad side.

Did **everyone** have a

good side?

Good side.

Bad side.

I wonder if the **best-looking** kid at school, Hans Some, has a bad side?

Nup.

Good side. ↓

VERY good side. ↓

I suppose it doesn't work with everyone. Maybe it's just **MY** family.

'Mum,' I said, 'you're **weird**.'

AND PROUD OF IT!

ACTION!

CHAPTER 3

We started following Joey everywhere...

and **filmed** everything he did. We still didn't know what it had to do with **FRIENDSHIP**... but we would worry about that later!

Joey loved **hopping** into the kitchen to eat FiDo's food. For one small roo, he had one **BIG** appetite!

MMMM-MMM.

He also liked **snuggling** up in FiDo's bed... Joey was so **cosy** in there, you'd think it was **HIS** bed!

Zzzzzzz

Joey **LOVED** Blockhead's toys...

He loved Blockhead's **favourite** spot on the couch too.

WHAT?!

We **loved** having Joey in our home...

but FiDo and Blockhead **weren't** happy at all!

HMPH!

RUFF!

They were probably **worried** that Joey was **TAKING OVER** their roles!

Not even Dad's jokes could **cheer** them up!

WHAT DO YOU CALL A KANGAROO ON TOP OF A HOUSE?

A KANGAROOF!

WHAT DO YOU GET WHEN YOU CROSS A KANGAROO WITH A SHEEP?

A WOOLLY JUMPER!

WHAT DO YOU GET WHEN YOU CROSS A KANGAROO WITH A TRUCK?

GREAT BIG HOLES DOWN THE STREET!

'Not even a **smile**?' said Dad.

HMPH! HMPH!

Mum helped Joey learn how to **survive** in nature, and I caught everything on film.

ACTION!

As Joey's foot got **better**, Roger showed him how to **hop**.

HOP! HOP! HIPPITY-HOP!

Sally fed him his **special** roo-food…
and **sang** him **silly** songs.

"RING-A-RING A ROO-SY…

Granddad wanted to help too. He **stitched** a **big pocket** onto his favourite overalls.

'I can carry Joey around in here and show him what it's like to be a baby roo,' he said.

SEE?
A POUCH!

Granddad reached into the **pouch** and dug around.

'And when Joey's busy,' he said, 'I can use the pocket for my **spare teeth!**'

SEE? TEETH POCKET!

Joey loved **hanging out** in Granddad's homemade pouch.

HOP, HOP, HOP!

'Hey,' said Granddad. **'Where did my teeth go?'**

HE HE HE!

I **wished** Joey could move in with us **for good**. Mum really liked him too.

YOU'RE SUCH A SWEET LITTLE ROO-BABY.

But I knew Joey had a **mum** out there that was missing him.

'How are we going to find Joey's mother?' I asked my mum.

'Yeah,' said Bella. 'The poor thing must be so **worried** about him.'

Mum said that Joey's mother had a **triangle-shaped tag** on her right ear. The tag would help us find her.

JUST LIKE THIS.

'We're going to start searching for her tomorrow afternoon using a special **tracking** device,' said Mum. 'It's kind of like a **metal detector**.'

'So it makes a **BEEPING** sound, the closer you get to the tag?' I asked.

'Yep.'

That sounded **really cool**. If only it could help me find all my missing socks.

RUN!

'We should go with Mum,' I said to Bella, 'and film it all. How about you do the **filming** tomorrow?'

'That sounds **perfect**,' said Bella.

TEAMWORK!

HUH?!

CHAPTER 4

We had heaps of **fun footage** of Joey... but we still hadn't started our **movie** about friendship!

'Why don't we try... looking up the definition of "friendship",' said Bella, handing me a **dictionary**.

WHOA.

I **flicked** to the right page and Bella started filming.

'The dictionary says that **friendship** is `the state of being a friend`,' I read.

The state of being a friend? **Huh?**

I'M IN THE STATE OF BEING CONFUSED.

'I don't even know what that means,' I said.

'Me neither,' said Bella. 'Geez, we're really **stuck** on how to make this film...'

Suddenly, Dad **popped** his head through the doorway.

COCK-A-DOODLE-ROO!

Dad showed us this **strange-looking** device.

It was the
triangle-tag tracker!

'I'm about to start the **search** for Joey's mum,' he said. 'Your mum can't come—she's caught up at the **animal hospital** with a **lizard** that accidentally bit his tongue.'

MY TONGUE ITH
REALLY
THORE!

'Do you two want to join me for the **hike**?' said Dad.

'Of course, we'll come!' I said. 'Right, Bella?'

'Yep,' she said. 'This **boring** ... I mean, **tough** ... friendship film will just have to wait. There's a baby roo that needs his mother!'

LET'S GO FIND HER!

Blockhead and FiDo were **NOT HAPPY** about staying home with Joey. But we needed them to keep an eye on him.

I **hoped** they could all **get along!**

WELL, WE'D BETTER **HOP** TO IT!

BLOOPER!

CHAPTER 5

We'd only been **hiking** for a little while when the tracker began **beeping!**

BEEP! BEEP! BEEP!

'IT'S BEEPING!' Dad shouted.

'Shh!' I whispered. 'You might **scare** the roo away!'

'Oops,' said Dad, in a **reeeeeally** loud whisper. 'It's **BEEEEPING!**'

FOLLOW ME!

Bella and I ran after Dad. I couldn't believe we'd almost found Joey's mum already. We'd barely even begun our **bush hike!**

Was it going to be that easy?

The beeping was growing **louder!**
　　　　I guess it **WAS** going to be that easy!

THAT WAY!

We were **running** after Dad, **leaping** logs, **dodging** rocks and **ducking** branches.

When suddenly...

SKIIIIIIIII

Dad **crashed** to a stop!

THUD!

And we **crashed** into him!

OOOOF!

We'd found the beeping.
 Only it **wasn't** coming from our tracker...

It was coming from... a cricket!

WELL, HELLO!

A CRICKET!

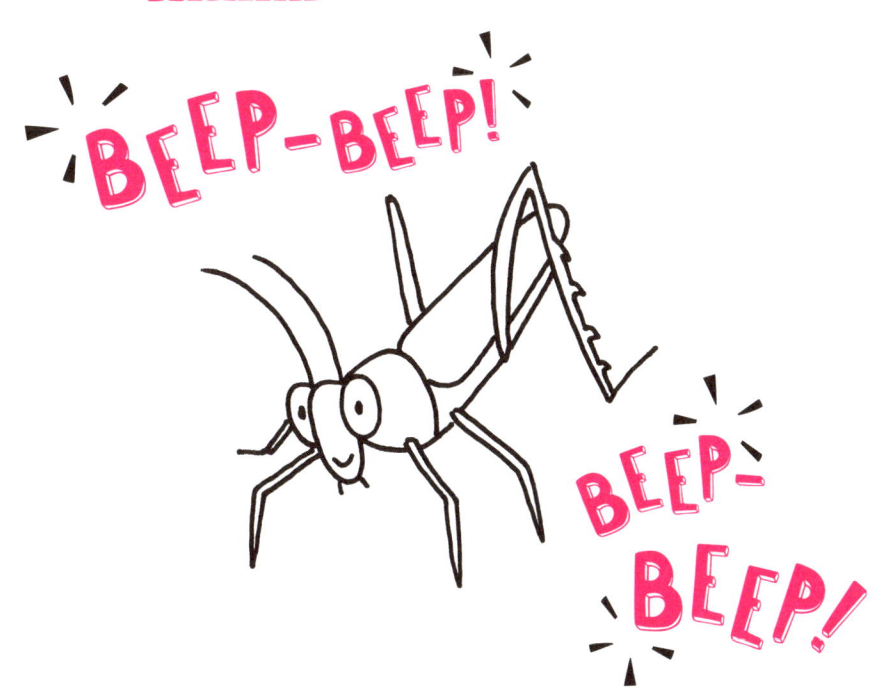

BEEP-BEEP!

BEEP-BEEP!

The cricket sounded just like the tracker!

Oh man. I should have known it wasn't going to be that **easy**!

'Wait a second,' said Bella. 'I think the tracker's **beeping** again.'

BEEP!

BEEP-BEEP!

Dad held the tracker up to his ear. 'Yep, I can hear it.'

'FOLLOW ME!'

Again, we chased after Dad.

This time we **jumped** over a creek...

squeeeezed through some bushes...

and carefully **stepped** down a grassy hill.

Well... **BELLA** carefully stepped down the hill.

Dad and I **TUMBLED.**

The only thing that stopped us from tumbling...

WHOA!

EEEEEK!

...was a tree.

oooOOF!

OUCH.

BEEP! BEEP!

We could still hear beeping,
loud and **clear!**

In fact, it was coming from up ↑↑ high.

Up high? I looked up.

BEEP!

Oh man! It was a **BIRD** making a beeping sound, not the tracker! We'd followed the wrong beep... **AGAIN!**

Could this hike get any **worse?**

PLOP!

Why do birds always POOP on me?!

'Hahaha,' Bella **laughed**. 'Got that on camera!'

THAT'S ONE FOR THE BLOOPER REEL!

'The sound on this tracker is not a great idea,' said Dad. 'There are too many **noises** in the bush that sound like **beeping!**'

He was right. At this rate we'd find every animal in the bush **EXCEPT** the kangaroo we were looking for!

But Dad thought he had a solution. He would **fix** the tracker so that it made a different sound.

Dad **disappeared** for a few moments behind a **BIG** bush.

BZZZZZ... BEEP-BEEP

We heard some **weird** muffled noises...
before he **jumped** out with a big **grin**.

LISTEN TO
THIS!

Dad held out the tracker and **pressed** a button.

BUUUUUUUUUUUURRRRRRRP!

The tracker burped! An **ENORMOUS, THUNDEROUS BURP!**

"WHAT WAS THAT?!"

"EARTHQUAKE! RUN!"

Bella and I **cracked up** laughing.

HAHA! HAHAHA!

'You're right, Mr Do,' said Bella. 'Surely we won't hear that anywhere else!'

We hiked for another hour or so... but the tracker didn't burp once. Joey's mum was **nowhere** to be found.

'We'd better go home,' said Dad, 'and check on how Blockhead, FiDo and Joey are getting along. Hopefully they haven't been **fighting** this whole time!'

Back at home, we got a **HUGE** shock.

You wouldn't believe what we found . . .

ZZZZZZZZZ

We had **no idea** what had happened while we were out, but it looked as though Blockhead and FiDo had finally become **friends** with Joey!

In fact, they looked like they'd become the very

♥**best of friends!**♥

When they woke up, FiDo and Joey **ate some oats** together...

MMM-MM.

they played with some **chew toys**...

MUNCH, CHEW-CHEW!

and watched some **'Funniest Animals'** on TV with Blockhead!

HAHA HAHA!

Bella was there to film it all!

Later, we sat down together and watched the cool footage. Bella had done an **awesome** job.

Except for one part I didn't like very much!

WHY DO BIRDS ALWAYS POOP ON ME?!

Bella laughed. It **WAS** pretty funny, I guess!

Everything we'd filmed was great ... but it still had **NOTHING** to do with friendship!

UGH! WHAT ARE WE GOING TO DO?!

We were **running out of time** to **finish our project!**

Meanwhile, I had to find something to take to school for **show-and-tell**. I didn't know what I was going to do for that either!

Until **Joey** hugged my leg...

PERFECT!

When Mum came home, I asked her if I could take **JOEY** to school.

'Pleeeeeease,' I begged. 'Everyone will love him. It'll be the best show-and-tell ever!'

Mum said **no** ...

SORRY, WEIR, BUT JOEY NEEDS HIS REST.

Luckily, I had another idea. What if I took the **tracker** to school?

I picked it up.

CAN I TAKE THIS? PLEEEE-EEEASE?

'OK, Weir,' said Mum. 'As long as you take **VERY** good care of it!'

BURP!

CHAPTER 6

For show-and-tell, Henry and Wendy brought in the **GIANT cupcake** they'd baked for their friendship film.

IT'S DELICIOUS!

AND NUTRITIOUS!

'I love chocolate,' said Henry, 'and Wendy loves banana. So we made a **chocolate-banana** cupcake!'

INTRODUCING THE CHOC-NANA CUPCAKE!

YUM!

Blake Green passed around a **shell** he found at the **beach**.

HERE YOU GO.

Toby **dropped** the shell and a **crab** came running out! In fact, it ran up his leg and **pinched** him on the **bottom!**

PINCH!

OUCH!

Bella brought in a piece of **toast** that looked like a **face**. It looked just like **Miss Franklin!**

GOOD MORNING, CLASS!

HAHA, IT DOES LOOK LIKE ME!

Finally, it was my turn. I pulled the **tracker** out of my **backpack**.

'This is a roo tracker,' I told the class. 'It's going to help us find a **lost** joey's mum—'

BURRRRRRRRRRRRRRRP!

'Goodness!' said Miss Franklin. **'Who was that?'**

Miss Franklin looked around the class, trying to find the **LOUD** burper!

But it wasn't someone in the class.

IT'S THE TRACKER!

And that meant **Joey's mum** was nearby!

'Dad fixed the tracker so that it **burps** the closer we get to Joey's mum,' I said. 'She must be **outside** somewhere!'

QUICK!
LET'S FIND HER!

BURP-BURP!

Bella picked up the **camera** and started filming. Miss Franklin and our **entire class** followed us outside.

BURP-BURRRRP! BURRRRRP!

The burping was getting *faster* and **LOUDER!** We were close!

BURRRRRP!

BURP-BURP-BURP!

BURRRRRRR

Over in the nearby bush there was a group of **kangaroos** eating grass.

I could see a **roo** with a **triangle tag** on her ear. 'There she is!' I shouted.

'That's her on the right!' said Bella.

RRRP!

tag

WE'D FOUND JOEY'S MUM!

Now I had to let **MY** mum know!

Bella and I raced home after school to tell Mum we'd found Joey's mother. We were **very excited**. Joey was going to be so happy!

'Mum! Dad!' I shouted. 'We found Joey's mum near our school!'

I thought everyone would cheer! Instead, Blockhead was **squawking**, FiDo was **barking** and Mum looked panicked. She was frantically **running** around the house!

'It's Joey!' she said.

WE **CAN'T** FIND HIM!

SNIFF!
SNIFF!

CHAPTER 7

Mum said the animals were playing hide-and-seek together, when Joey completely **VANISHED.**

We turned the house **upside down** looking for him!

NOPE, NO JOEY!

He was nowhere to be found!

Mum and Dad searched **upstairs**.

Sally, Granddad and Roger searched **downstairs**.

Bella and I searched out the **back**.

And Blockhead and FiDo searched out the **front**.

JOOOOO-EEEEEEEY!

We'd just about looked everywhere, when I had an **idea**.

Joey had been eating FiDo's oats. What if FiDo could track him down by **following the smell** of oats?

FiDo was great at tracking things down with his sense of smell.

He once found Granddad's **teeth** in a pile of old **smelly shoes!**

'FiDo,' I called out. 'You need to follow the scent of **OATS!**'

I quickly **grabbed** his food bowl so he could have a good **sniff**.

SNIFF!

Then we were off!

FiDo **BOLTED** towards the smell of the oats. Blockhead flapped and squawked above him. They were **desperate** to find their new friend.

FiDo ran down the **driveway** and out to the pavement. He turned and ran a bit further, before **running** right up **BELLA'S** driveway!

'He's running into my house?!' said Bella, opening the door for FiDo.

'Ruff!' said FiDo.

FiDo ran inside and straight to Bella's **bedroom**. Blockhead was right behind him.

'JOEY!' Blockhead **cried** out.

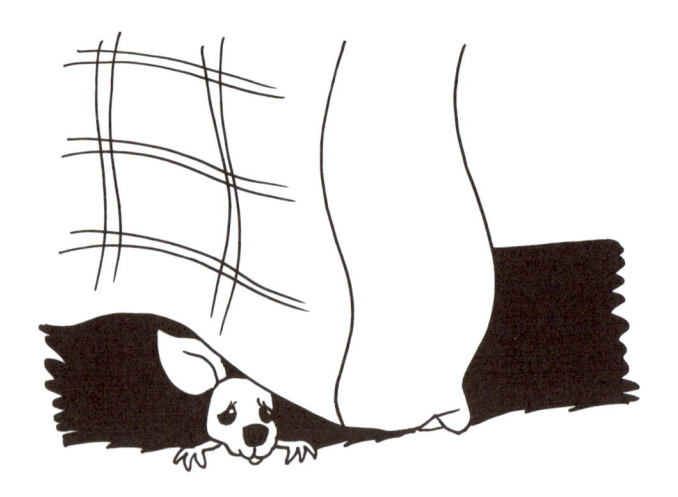

'There he is!' I said, pointing **under the bed**.

Joey came out, **jumped** into my arms and gave me a **big lick** on the face!

'You gave us quite a scare, little fella,' I said.

I had to admit, he was **SERIOUSLY** good at playing hide-and-seek.

Everyone was **SO HAPPY** to have found Joey again. But no-one was happier than Blockhead and FiDo.

BFFs! BEST FRIENDS FOREVER!

'Look,' said Mum, pulling off Joey's loose bandage. 'Joey's foot has completely healed!'

It was true, Joey's foot looked as **good as new!**

NOW LET'S GO FIND HIS MUM!

WASN'T ME!

CHAPTER 8

We headed back to school. Henry and Wendy joined us too, while Granddad carried Joey in his homemade **roo pouch**.

I led everyone to the **grassy spot** where we last saw Joey's mum.

'She was just over there,' I said, pointing.

But the **kangaroos** had moved on.

JUST ME HERE!

BURRRRRP!

We heard a really loud **BURP!** The roo must have been close!

BUUUURRRRP!
BURRRRRRRRRP!

'Excuse me!' said Henry.

HIC!
BURRRRP!

'Oops,' he said. 'This **cupcake** is making me burp!'

BURRRRRRP!

'Maybe you could save the rest for later?' said Bella.

'Good idea,' said Henry.

Just as Henry was **stuffing** the rest of the cupcake into his pocket, we heard **another** big BURP!

BURRRRRRP!
BURP-BURP!

'Wasn't me!' said Henry.

'It was the tracker!' said Dad.

LET'S GO!

Luckily, it wasn't long before we found the group of roos. They were a little bit closer to the bush this time. The tracker went **wild!**

BURP! BURP! BURP! BURP! BURP!

I carefully lifted Joey out of Granddad's pouch and **popped** him on the ground.

When Joey's mum saw him there,
she instantly **leapt** over to him.

Joey **beamed** with happiness and **hugged** his mum tight.

Joey's mum looked at us with big, warm eyes.
I think she was trying to say

THANK YOU!

It felt so good seeing Joey and his mum back together... but I couldn't help feeling a bit **sad** too. It was time for us to say **goodbye**.

Poor Blockhead and FiDo looked the **saddest** of all!

SOB! SOB!

Joey **hopped** over to say goodbye to us.
We all took turns giving him a **cuddle**.

BYE, BUDDY!

Blockhead gave Joey a **huge hug**, while FiDo gave him a few wet **licks**.

And then it was time for Joey to go. He hopped into his mum's pouch, then they **bounced** back into the bush together.

Blockhead and FiDo looked so sad ...

I turned to Bella.

'They're really going to miss their **new friend**,' I said.

'They sure are,' said Bella.

Then, **FINALLY**, the idea for our film hit us at the exact same time.

WE SHOULD MAKE THE FILM ABOUT NEW FRIENDS— BLOCKHEAD, FIDO AND JOEY!

YES!

A film about **friendship** with a **kangaroo!**

WORTH IT!

CHAPTER 9

We loved sharing our **friendship film** with the class. We put together all of our best footage, and I even added a few **cool** fold-ins.

A BIRD, A DOG AND A ROO

A Story of Friendship

Our film showed how Blockhead and FiDo weren't so sure about their new house guest, at first.

...Joey ate their food. **snuck** into their beds...

chewed their toys...

and took their **favourite spots** on the couch.

WHAT?!

But soon, they realised they could **learn** a lot from each other.

'FiDo helped Joey with his **hopping**...'

A

B Fold line B over to meet line A

'Blockhead taught him how to **box**...'

A

142

B And again!

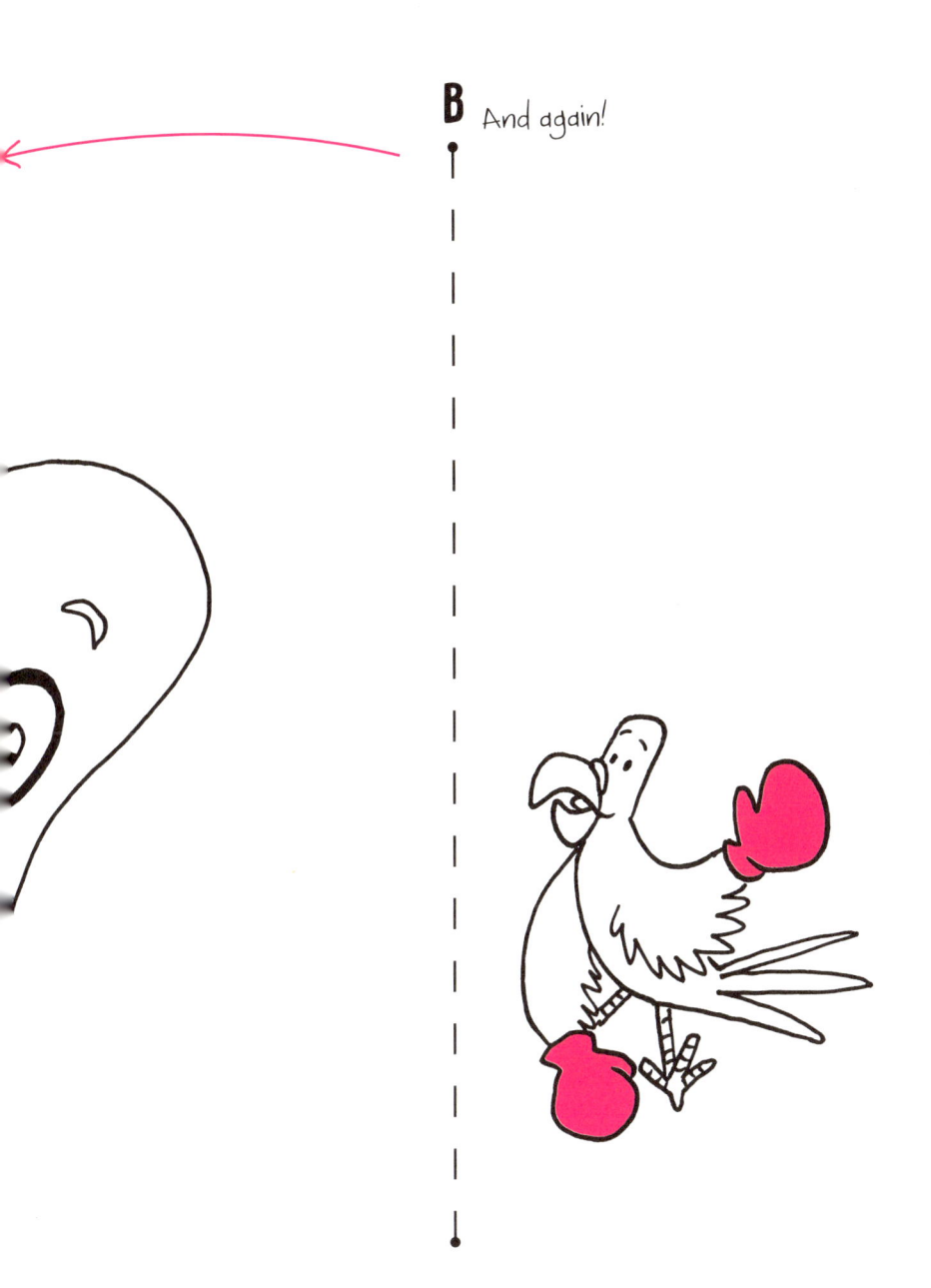

Joey taught them both how to **share**...

and soon they became **best friends**.

Even though it was really sad for the new friends to say goodbye...

...it was worth it.

And Blockhead and FiDo learned the **greatest** friendship lesson of all.

There's always room for

EVERYONE!"

The whole class started **clapping** and **cheering**.

Our short film was a hit!

MUM, I'M A **MOVIE STAR!**

AUSTRALIAN BOOK INDUSTRY AWARDS WINNER!
Book 1
GOT IT!
ANH DO
WEIRDO
2014
ABIA
WINNER
SCHOLASTIC
bird
Book 2
GOT IT!
WEIRDO 2
EVEN WEIRDER!
ANH DO
SCHOLASTIC

ladybug!

COLLECT THEM ALL!

ANH DO — WEIRDO 3: EXTRA WEIRD!

Book 3

GOT IT!

gnomes

flying soccer ball

COLLECT THEM ALL!

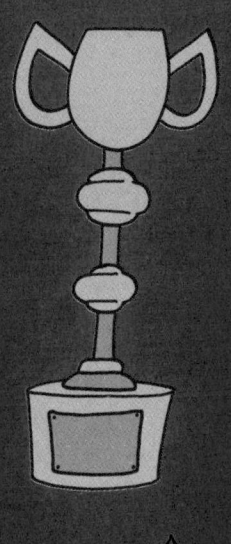

trophy ↗

← Book 4

GOT IT!

pet rock ↓

pineapple ←

Book 5 → **GOT IT!**

Book 6 → **GOT IT!**

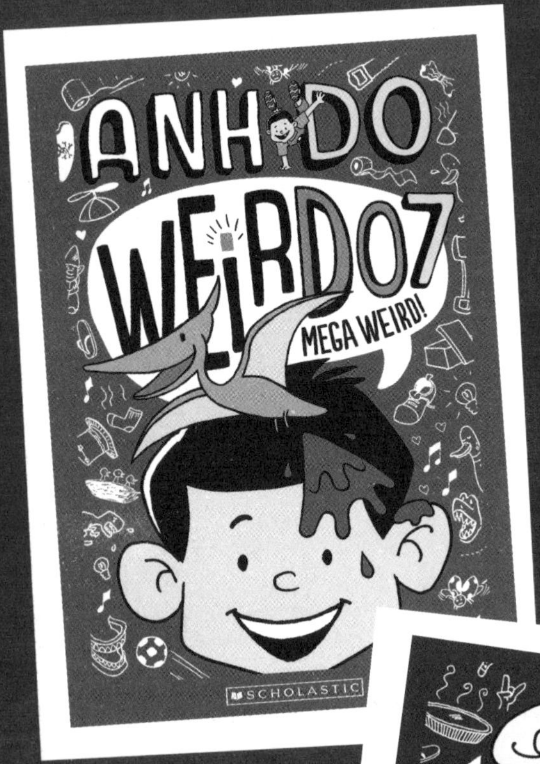

Book 7

GOT IT!

pig

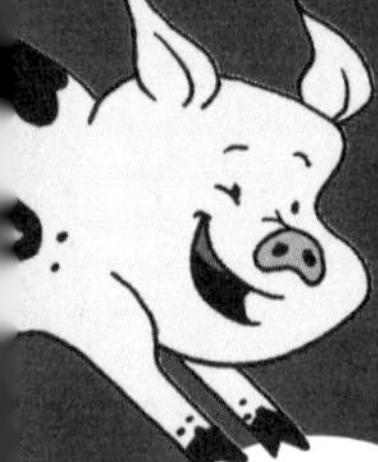

Book 8

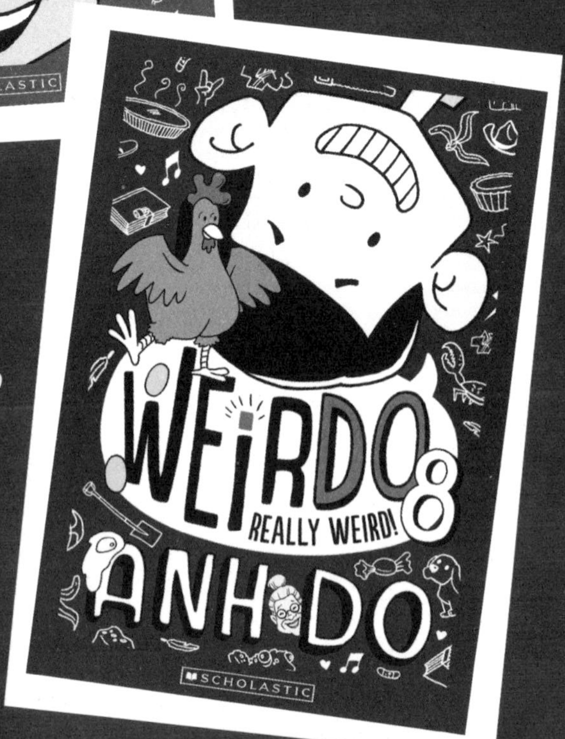

GOT IT!

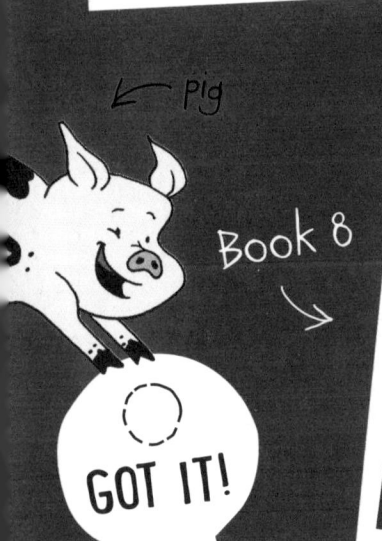

spider!

COLLECT THEM ALL!

ANH DO
WEIRDO 9
SPOOKY WEIRD!

Book 9

GOT IT!

Roger

grapes

COLLECT THEM ALL!

Book 10 ↓

WEiRDO 10
MESSY WEIRD!
ANH DO

GOT IT!

Book 11 ↓

GOT IT!

↑ worm

ANH DO
WEiRDO 11
SPLASHY WEIRD!